A FERRY TO CATCH

Daufuskie Island

By Carol Bellhouse

Photographs by Carol Bellhouse
and Lem Chesher

Copyright 2016 Carol Bellhouse

Published by Zuni Canyon Institute

Feel free to use short excerpts of this book for critique or review purposes. All other rights reserved. For more information and other queries, contact CarolBellhouse@gmail.com.

Chapter 1

"I'll call you back. I've got a ferry to catch."

"To where?" my best friend asks on the phone.

"Daufuskie Island."

"Where's that?" she asks.

"Off the coast of South Carolina. No roads or bridges to it. Can only get there by boat. Bye!"

I don't wait for her goodbye. Close friends are all right with that.

I throw my cell phone on the bed with its green blanket. I'm spending a week in a Hilton Head hotel on a well-deserved vacation. Chicago, my home, is a long way from here.

There are only four ferries to Daufuskie from Hilton Head every day. I made no attempt at the 6:30 a.m. departure, choosing to sleep in. I don't want to miss the 11:00. The last one returns at 5:30 in the evening so my time there will be short.

I stuff my sun hat, camera and money pouch into the daypack. Grabbing the phone and car key, I race out the door, remembering the keycard just before it closes on me. I don't feel like waiting for the elevator so I run down the stairs to the rental car.

This vacation is supposed to be one of my wild adventures. The Army and paramedic school were wild adventures. I'm prone to wild adventures like some people are prone to colds. Other people get the sniffles. I get adventures. I have a susceptibility to them in my blood, in my DNA, in my frontal lobe.

And besides, I think, *I've earned this trip.* I'm exhausted from long hours on the ambulance. After five years there are nights when I don't think I can do even one more shift.

Feeling desperately fatigued, both physically and emotionally, has led me here. I need to enlarge my vision beyond the flashing emergency lights of crisis.

My all-consuming profession, where every second and every movement count, has narrowed my consciousness to a pinpoint--the precise urgency of life or death.

I knew how tired and burned out I really was when I slept the whole flight to get here.

I drive the seven miles to the dock with my foot hard on the accelerator. Old habits die hard even on vacation, even in slower Southern latitudes.

I find the dirt lot and park the car, clicking the

remote twice to make sure the doors are locked.

Running to the ticket counter, the lady with orange hair smiles warmly at me. "Slow down," she says. "Boarding has started but you've got plenty of time."

I make a mental note to try walking for a change. Paying my money and receiving my ticket, I thank the woman and stroll to the wooden walkway. I remind myself to enjoy the day without rushing.

Daufuskie, here I come.

Chapter 2

Walking down the wooden pier, I admire the salt marshes, noting that it's high tide. The marshes have filled, flush with small marine life seeking refuge from the rolling waves of the Atlantic Ocean.

Turtles are probably in residence, along with crabs—ghost crabs with their long legs, tiny fiddler crabs, hermit crabs trading up in shell real estate, stone crabs with strong claws and blue crabs with their markings—the male apron shaped like the Washington Monument, the female like the Capitol Dome.

There are undoubtedly horseshoe crabs. I recall the first time I encountered a horseshoe crab. I was seven years old on a brief visit to Florida with my parents and younger brother.

I had noticed a rock slowly moving in the estuary flowing to the ocean. I watched it for a moment before realizing it was crawling under its own power and not just rolling in the water.

When I saw its ferociously spiny tail, I jumped away from it.

Enthralled and cautious, I waved over my brother and pointed.

"Ewww," he said. "What is it?"

"I thought it was a rock."

"Is it alive?" He took a step toward it.

I grabbed his arm. "Don't touch it."

"It has eyes!" he shouted in horror.

"Where?"

"One there," he pointed. "And there's the other one."

I peered at the creature, making out the eyes that looked like the barnacles covering its shell.

We followed it in the shallow water draining back to the ocean, charting its laborious progress and keeping well away from its scary tail.

It was quite a thrill for two young children to encounter a prehistoric creature while on a family trip.

I have never forgotten it.

Now I know they're not crabs at all. They're related to spiders. They're huge spiders in shells.

And they play a very important role in medicine. I know this also now, being in the medical field.

Biological researchers use the blood of horseshoe crabs to test for drug impurities. Their blood is very sensitive to bacteria and can detect any compromised pharmaceuticals.

Being rare, the horseshoe crab's blood is harvested without killing it. It's trapped, tapped for its blood and returned to the water alive.

Perfect blood donors.

Chapter 3

"Welcome aboard," says the deck hand, taking my ticket.

"Beautiful day," I tell him.

"It most certainly is," he drawls. He is as deep South as they come. "Ya'll have a good day."

The ferry is a small boat with two decks. It's old and worn and comfortable.

I could buy food at the little bar but there's no reason to. I cooked a big breakfast of steak and eggs before I got on the phone with my friend, before I raced to the dock and boarded.

I have a bottle of water in my day pack and don't want to miss a minute of being on deck. The air smells fresh and salty, so different from the smells of the city.

I look at my fellow passengers, mostly at their feet. I'm not often on a boat, so their footwear interests me. It tells me a little about who they are.

After touring the top deck, I descend to the main deck. I don't dare stay up top. The exaggerated roll there would prove to be too much for my stomach over the next hour.

I find a place to stand at the railing on the starboard side of the main deck and savor the ocean breeze.

I listen to the conversations around me.

"Did you remember the sunscreen?"

"These houses are awesome. Can you imagine having the money to live like that?"

"When can we go?"

"Be patient, Jimmy."

Waiting for departure, an Asian woman stands at the top of the stairs, looking expectantly across the water. Her tall partner has his arms around her with his hands clasping the rail.

The ocean wind blows and everyone settles in for the voyage.

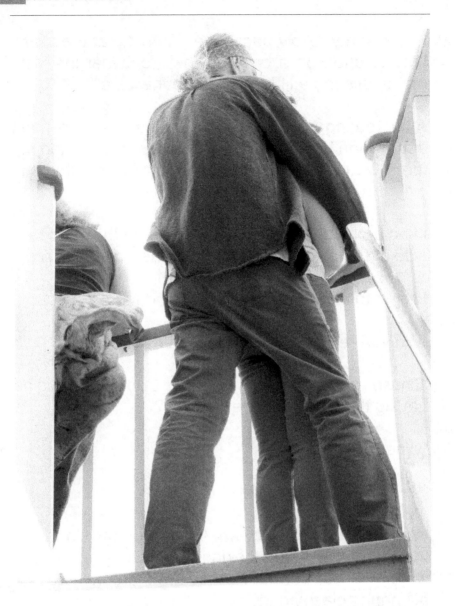

And then the engines fire up, the ropes are undone from the dock and we are underway.

A Ferry to Catch

Chapter 4

On the journey out of the harbor, we pass a crane repairing a boat dock. The piece of equipment does not reach from the shore to the dock. It's floating on a barge. I try to fathom how it can operate from a bobbing, buoyant surface but we're past it before I have time to figure it out.

The barrier islands of South Carolina protect the coastline from the onslaught of the Atlantic Ocean. It's my first time here and as always, I studied up on the place before I booked my flight. I know about the riptides and undertows but since it's only April, I won't be venturing into the water much above my ankles.

We pass under a bridge supporting the new trans-island parkway. His mother instructs Jimmy to listen to the cars overhead.

At the mouth of the harbor, pelicans line a concrete wall, watching for lunch. We pass on osprey nest perched defensively on top of a pole.

"The tides fluctuate eight feet here," a man's voice says.

I realize he's addressing me.

I turn toward the voice. I can only assume he's been watching me as I've been looking out across the bow.

He has blue eyes.

A Ferry to Catch

Chapter 5

"Eight feet is substantial," I respond.

He's tan and wears a hat that casts a shadow across his handsome, clean-shaven face. He has a dimple in his right cheek. I can see it even before he smiles, which he does when movement in the water catches his eye.

He gestures with his head. "Here comes a dolphin to ride our bow wake."

I turn my head and see the dolphin heading straight for us. I swear if a dolphin could look mischievous, this one does.

I don't know what's about to happen but I can tell it's going to be good.

I shrug out of my day pack and pull out my camera. I drop the pack to the deck and turn my attention to the gadgetry while keeping an eye on the approaching dolphin. I excitedly wait for the camera to boot up.

I elbow my way discreetly to the railing at the bow and lean over. I watch the dolphin disappear under the boat and then reappear, surfing the boat's front wake.

A Ferry to Catch 21

My finger on the shutter button, I take as many pictures as I can fire off.

Gray and sleek, the dolphin starts low in the water under the bow and then rides the wave to the right. She cuts back to the center of the boat, using the boat's propulsion to make a joyful jump before submerging and starting over again.

It's delightful and playful and I fall in love with the dolphin then and there. She's such a joyful creature, full of life.

The passengers standing at the bow of the ferry appreciate the show, pointing and exclaiming.

"Look at the dolphin, Jimmy!"

"That's so cool!"

The dolphin body-surfs twenty times before she tires of the game and swims away, content and happy, at least for the moment.

I turn to thank the man but he's gone. I realize I turned my back on him and left him standing at the railing.

If I see him again, I will thank him.

Chapter 6

Passing a buoy marked 31, we're in open water and have left the shelter of the harbor.

The ocean folds out across the horizon. I tip my head back and watch the pelicans and cormorants flying across the pale blue sky.

This is perfect, I think. A perfect day. A thousand

miles away from the sirens of Chicago.

A sailboat goes by and I admire the vessel's sleek lines. I imagine the sound of the wind on board instead of the noise of the ferry engine.

I glance around at my fellow passengers, hoping to

catch a glimpse of the mystery man with blue eyes and dimple but he's nowhere to be seen.

All of them, on the ferry headed to an island--I wonder what their stories might be. A good many are probably locals, using the ferry like mainlanders use the bus.

A few may be newlyweds; others, retirees taking the trip of their dreams, maybe even thinking about settling here on the South Carolina coast. A few Europeans may be at the start of a trip across the States.

I wonder about their stories and their scars.

When a plume of smoke appears on a tiny island,

the conversations of the passengers shift to it.

"Mom, what's that smoke?"

"I don't know, honey. Let's hope it's nothing serious."

I open my mouth to reassure the boy but stop when I hear a familiar voice.

"They're burning slash. Old leaves and broken branches," the voice says to the boy. "It's under control. Just a lot of smoke."

He's back.

"That island is private." His voice comes from behind me.

He's speaking to me now. "Some guy owns it but he's not around much. Caretaker's doing spring cleanup."

Holding onto the rail, I turn toward him, taking in his khaki pants, long legs and the dark blue t-shirt showing taut arms. "Thank you for the dolphin."

"You're welcome." He stands looking at me. He's in no hurry to go anywhere. He doesn't have many options.

We're on a ferry together in the Atlantic Ocean, heading for Daufuskie Island.

Chapter 7

"Want a tour of the boat?" he asks.

I like his flirty eyes. "You know this boat pretty well?"

"I should. I'm on it at least three times a month. Come on."

He sweeps his hand toward the main cabin and I'm off on a guided tour of everything aboard. He fawns over each nautical accoutrement.

I enjoy his humor immensely. I like the way he has fun with what he is obviously doing to pass the time.

He elaborates on the sea-washed windows and the painted railings like it's the Queen Mary. He points out the artistic composition of the ropes and hoses.

I play along, acting profoundly interested and impressed, which I can tell he appreciates.

It is actually the silliest tour ever taken and ever given, which we both know.

He points and pontificates and when he's not looking, I admire him in addition to the boat. I don't usually respond to male attention—not anymore. I'm too tired for anything but work.

But I'm on vacation and my defenses are down. I've slept well and there are no sirens.

"And here's the helm. Or steering wheel as we nautical experts call it."

"This is how they steer the boat?" I bat my eyelashes at him and wobble my head appropriately.

"Yes, little lady, that right there is how it's done."

The tour is short and fanciful, taking all of ten minutes, including the paddlewheel which is for show only.

And now we're back where we started," he announces after the spin around both decks leaves us smiling.

"That was the most amazing tour I've ever taken," I gush.

"Glad to be of service," he says.

"Do I tip you now or later?"

"Later. Much later. In fact, no tip is expected unless I deposit you on dry land alive."

He makes me laugh and I like that.

"Is there a chance of that not happening?"

"I'm afraid so," he leans into me and I catch a heady whiff of his skin. "Pirates," he whispers conspiratorially.

"P-Pirates?" I stutter to keep from guffawing.

"The most notorious pirate of all of pirate-dom plies these very waters."

"Have I ever heard of him?"

"We rarely speak his name aloud. But I will whisper it to you since your life may depend on it."

"Oh, good sir," I swoon. "Dare tell!"

He brushes aside my hair with a finger and moves his lips close to my ear.

I can feel his warm breath tickling my earlobe and neck. My knees go weak and I grab the railing.

I close my eyes and listen to the name. "Floyd Fluffy. The Third."

That's when I start to giggle and can't stop.

He smiles happily at his success. "You are sworn to secrecy."

"Absolutely," I gasp. "I'll never breathe a word to anyone. It would cause panic."

"I knew I could trust you. I'm a brilliant judge of character."

"How do you know all these important secrets? And why are you on this ferry so much?" I ask.

A Ferry to Catch

"I live on Daufuskie."

Chapter 8

He doesn't have a southern accent and can tell by my quizzical look what my question will be.

A Ferry to Catch

He laughs. "Not originally. My place of origin is a cattle ranch in Nebraska. Although we also grew hay, which may qualify it as a farm. I guess I should make up my mind sooner or later."

"Whether you're a farm boy or a ranch kid?"

"Rightly so. Nice place to grow up. Occasionally visit. And stay as far away as I can the rest of the time."

"That's okay," I reply. "Here's my confession—I'm from Springfield, Illinois, currently residing in Chicago. I have nightmares about being surrounded by a thousand miles of cornfields in every direction."

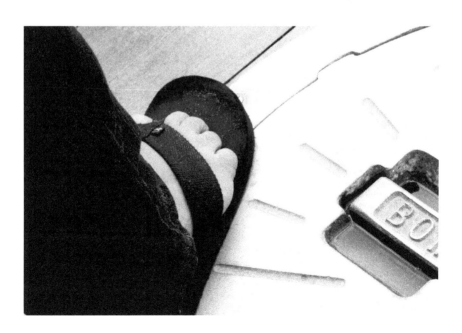

He nods in agreement. He understands. "The American Midwest. Where it's either too hot or too cold or it's raining. And the people are the salt of the earth."

I can't help but laugh. "So true. So true."

"Right?" He smiles.

I find his chuckle disarming. It's throaty and genuine and I like how easily it ripples up from him.

"So how did you come to be on an island in the Atlantic?"

"I caretake a property. And I'm writing a novel. And in my spare time, I sometimes work as a tour guide. When I feel so inclined."

"So I'm the beneficiary of your inclination to give a tour?"

"And since I'm on a roll, I could be talked into providing a personal tour of this lovely island we're approaching."

And that's when I hesitate.

A Ferry to Catch   41

Chapter 9

The ferry slows and approaches the dock of the island. This must be Daufuskie.

A Ferry to Catch

The river continues upstream, disappearing around a bend. It's the shipping channel that leads to Savannah.

My thoughts are racing in expanding loops inside my brain. It's one thing to take a tour of a small boat on which there are fifty people. It's another to agree to a private tour of a sparsely-populated island.

"I have a–I–. A golf cart for the day was included with my ticket."

"That's okay. I have my own golf cart. We can be a gang."

I ponder how sparse a sparsely-populated island is in reality. I've seen other passengers onboard with golf-cart vouchers and island maps with X's marked on them directing them to places to see.

I weigh it quickly in my head, a statistical analysis of danger versus adventure. And, as usually happens in my case, instead of getting the sniffles, I come down with a case of Wild Adventure.

He makes me just giddy enough to want more of the feeling. I'd like to catch another whiff of his skin and maybe the thrill of another secret whispered into my ear.

"Sure," I hear myself say. "Why not?"

The captain works the engines—forward, reverse, forward, reverse—as he slows the boat and it floats sideways toward the dock.

I watch the process from the railing, feeling the man's slight smile beside me.

The deck hand with the strong accent, a local boy for certain, jumps from the boat onto the boards and works his magic in tying up.

The captain cuts the engines.

The conversations onboard pick up in the silence.

"We sure picked a nice day."

"Where's the water bottle?"

"Let's have lunch before we head to the house."

I'm looking across the dock at an extravagantly broken-down pier dipping and sliding precariously into the salt water.

The island is lush and green and inviting.

I turn to the man, my tour-guide and swashbuckler.

"What's your name?" I ask.

"Miles. Miles Enfield."

"I'm Elizabeth. Elizabeth Dunne."

A Ferry to Catch

Chapter 10

My rented golf cart has a speed governor so it won't go over fifteen miles per hour, I'm told as I sign the waiver.

Miles has loaded his supplies from the ferry onto a golf cart parked at the dock. I assume he owns it or maybe it belongs to the property he caretakes.

I'm sure his cart can run circles around mine in top end but I like the independence of piloting my own machine.

"Ready?" he asks. "No wheelies allowed. At least in

view of the rental shop."

We start out, following the other rental carts.

I know Miles is sticking close to the others for my benefit and I appreciate his consideration.

I get the hang of the cart quickly, having driven similar ones for my father on his golf outings after he injured his leg in the car accident.

When I left for college, he stopped golfing. I wonder, in the moment, my hands on the steering wheel, if it was because I wasn't there to drive him any longer.

On golfing days, our talks were interrupted only by the whipping sound of the club as I sat waiting for him. He wanted to teach me to play but I always laughed and replied, "I'm not old enough, Dad. I'll take lessons when I'm sixty!"

We still talk on Sundays but it's by phone now, over the miles. The digital conversations will never take the place of our heart-to-heart discussions on the golf course.

Part of the reserve for both of us is that my mother is listening, excited for her turn, reaching for the phone. It's not that there's anything wrong with my mother. It's just that the flow of our conversation doesn't have the open-air quality it had when we were cruising the greens–just the two of us.

I wonder if he misses our conversations from the old days as much as I do.

The golf-carts ahead of us turn into a cemetery

near the docks and overlooking the ocean.

"Look at the Spanish moss!" I yell across to Miles.

I've never been anywhere with a thicker display. It drapes from the trees like a fabric, ethereal and weightless. Not even Hilton Head has this.

I know Spanish moss is an air plant. So when Miles opens his mouth to start into his riff, I interrupt him and smile. "And it's not parasitic on the tree."

He looks at me with surprise and admiration. When I wink and laugh, he shoots back, "Own it, girl!"

We pull our carts alongside the others and turn off the engines.

He jumps out to help me climb from mine, which I find endearing. My heart does a funny dance when I put my hand in his.

I thank him profusely and I mean it. Golf carts do not allow for dignified exits.

I pull my sun hat from my pack and drop it on my head. I can't wait to explore the history of this cemetery-by-the-sea.

"Ready?" asks Miles, gesturing.

"Of course!"

"I don't see any poison ivy but we're bound to get into it somewhere."

"Didn't I hear you advertise this as a non-lethal tour?"

Miles chuckles and I feel a warm spot of happiness

spread through my belly.

"I've never heard of poison ivy being lethal but I suppose there's always a first time."

"I hear it's a horrible way to die," I begin spinning my own outlandish tale. "With skin eruptions and bleeding from the eyes and convulsions that break your bones."

Miles hesitates for a moment and then laughs as he realizes I like telling outrageous stories as much as he does. Floyd Fluffy the Third indeed.

We wander through the trees. The cemetery is wondrous--unkempt with headstones heaved and askew.

The proximity to the water is intoxicating. The grave markers, their granite eaten away by the sea air, are mysterious and majestic in their obscurity.

Wisps of clouds make an appearance across the sky.

We're careful of tree roots and watch for poison ivy, especially after my dire prediction.

Miles and I are silent, overhearing the occasional comment from the others.

"1902."

"Can you read that? Adam Stevenson?"

"I can't make out this one at all."

"What a lovely place to be buried."

Although I don't respond to the comment, I couldn't agree more.

I look at Miles and smile.

Chapter 11

The group begins to break up and dissipate, headed to different points of interest, in search of the X's marked on the maps.

Some leave the cemetery quickly, making a quick pass around the markers and hopping back in their golf carts.

There's is a group of three left when Miles turns to me and says, "There are three cemeteries on the island. Want to see the other two?"

I love cemeteries. I find them peaceful and pastoral and elegant, no matter how neglected or downtrodden.

"Oh yes, let's go."

Firing up our carts, we hit the road again, passing milky ponds in the trees layered with tangled vines and ferns.

I make a note to ask Miles why the swamp water is so white.

I figure he'll know, and if he doesn't, he'll make up something funny.

The second cemetery is inland from the sea and, as a result, the greenery is more dense.

An older couple from the boat is already there, speaking more loudly than is called for. As we approach, they hop in their golf cart and move on, leaving a wonderful silence behind.

Miles and I wander slowly among the headstones, occasionally pointing out something to each other or reading the names or dates out loud.

"This one was young—only twelve."

"A hundred years ago…"

Time becomes suspended and I don't realize I'm hungry until we return to the carts.

Miles is one step ahead of me, digging under the supply boxes piled in his cart--power tools and paper towels and groceries.

He comes up with a box of snacks–tuna salad, cheese and crackers. He raises his eyebrows in invitation. "Will this do?"

I nod heartily. "It will more than do! It's perfect."

We sit in his golf cart and open the individual packages, taking in the day and enjoying our lunch.

Our conversation is unhurried.

"Good?"

"Delicious."

The island is getting under our skin, the quiet and lushness easing the need to make small talk.

So when another golf cart pulls up with loud voices and harsh laughter, we simply look at each other, start our individual carts, and move on.

Chapter 12

Trucks and cars do exist on the island.

"Not many," explains Miles. "They have to be brought over by boat."

"And that's expensive, right?"

"Yes. A real hassle."

"Without many places to go, anyway."

"It's an island, for sure."

On the way to the third cemetery, Miles pulls his cart to the side of the primitive road and turns off the key.

I stop behind him.

He jumps out and walks back to me. "I found this one day when I was exploring."

"Found what?" I ask, looking around.

"That." He points to a forlornly abandoned house, more of a shack, in the trees.

"Oh my." I would not have seen it on my own.

Miles moves into the bushes toward the structure. "Come on."

"Absolutely!" I grab my camera and follow him.

"Poison ivy." He points so I can avoid it.

"Is this a Gullah house?" I ask.

Miles stops and turns his head to look at me. "What do you know about the Gullah?"

"That they've lived here since the Civil War."

"You know the history? These islands were the first to be taken by the Union soldiers when the war started. They knew they could squeeze off supply lines by controlling the islands and the waterways."

"And it was a successful strategy?"

"Probably won the war. The plantation owners headed south and inland, leaving everything behind. Including their slaves. First freed slaves of the Emancipation."

"And they stayed. Establishing their own world—customs, language, community." I know enough of the story to be fascinated by it.

"Not many people know anything about them. How cut off they were from the mainland and how preserved and pristine it was until the developers arrived. How do you know about them?"

I shrug. "Research. What's happened to them since the developers got here?"

"Lot of things. They got priced off their land and left for work on the mainland. And since they didn't identify themselves as Gullah or Geechee..."

"Why not?"

"Because it was not a compliment back then. They were just people living on the island. People like Jake and Flossie Washington. Lawrence Jenkins. Big Dick Johnson. You know the story about scrap iron, don't you?"

"I don't think so."

"They loaded their boats with moonshine to sell in Savannah and put scrap iron over it. They knew a revenue officer would stop them somewhere along the way. Ask what they were hauling. They'd say, 'Scrap iron. Need to feed the children.' A load of scrap iron. There's a local drink still called that."

I like the story. "Scrap iron," I repeat.

"The history of this place," he sighs. "And all the stories being lost."

We stand looking at the sagging and shattered house, wondering, envisioning who had lived there and what life had been like.

And then it's like a metal door slides over his face.

Chapter 13

An expression of coldness and anger obliterates the smile, the dimple and the sparkle in his eyes.

Something has touched a nerve in him. Something about the island. Or the Gullah people. Or the developers who have brought so much change to this place.

He must feel deeply to account for the anguish I see all over his face.

I don't know what to say. I turn away, looking at the veiled trees and dense underbrush. I don't want to intrude on his emotions. A wave of panic surges through my blood. I try to wait it out, hoping it will pass over like a storm cloud.

I want to believe that this, whatever it is, is not about me. *Or at least I hope it's not.*

Since I don't know what's just happened, I fall back on my professional training. I wait. I give it time. I don't push my way in. I don't impose myself on it.

I wait some more.

"Yeah. Well." Miles looks at me to see if I'm ready to go.

I nod and he turns back toward the carts.

He takes a step and then turns toward me again. "It's not you."

I look at his face and nod. "I know."

Chapter 14

"This is the third and last cemetery," Miles announces as we pull up to the wrought-iron gate.

It's been a quiet drive over in the golf carts.

His sudden transformation from a lighthearted companion to a moody, withdrawn being unsettles me.

I have had my share of moody men.

There was the boyfriend who preferred to watch TV over anything else in life, including spending time with me. Another could shift gears on his emotions in the middle of a sentence. The most recent one yelled during conversations to show his passion about the subject.

They had all been loved and left. I don't mind men honoring their emotions. But I am worn out from being on the receiving end of the egocentric rollercoaster ride.

I've decided it's just not my cup of tea.

So I have wished them well, one and all, and I've gone my own way.

I've been out of love now for almost two years. I've had enough to know I'm much happier alone than with a moody man.

Miles doesn't help me from my cart at the cemetery. He doesn't wait for me. He turns off his ignition and walks away without me.

I sit in my cart for a moment, inspecting a well pump while I watch him from the corner of my eye.

Uncertain, I climb out of the cart and move toward the headstones. I keep my distance from the lone figure who has become someone else, a stranger.

The flowers are lovely, languidly draping the small, walled area. A green lizard pauses on a headstone among the leaves left from autumn.

I admire the moss growing on the brick mausoleum.

And then I take my leave.

I call out to Miles, who is staring solemnly at a faded grave marker. "I'm going to catch up with the group. Thank you for the tours and lunch."

I considered saying nothing, simply driving away. I feel better departing on a softer note. I wave my hand because I don't know what else to do.

I walk to my cart, glancing back only once to see him standing still, his arms hanging at his side, with no emotion at all on his face.

Chapter 15

I drive away as quickly as my limited horsepower will take me, turning onto different roads before pulling over to calm the knot in my stomach and extract the map from my pack.

I look at the red X's. I find reassurance in knowing where the others will be—to find them or avoid them.

It's obvious I can't get lost on a small island without major effort, so I determine north from the shadows and step on the gas.

I head in the direction of the undertaker's house, reading the story of the undertaker marrying the midwife, giving rise to the joke, "She brought them in and he took them out."

I slow to admire the unique houses, island homes in various states of disrepair. Some are abandoned and some are still occupied.

There's a white house with blue shutters and a red house with white shutters. The house with the rusted tin roof sports dilapidated green shutters. The house with the blue roof has no shutters at all.

I want to pat myself on the back and offer words of encouragement. For once, I haven't dedicated months or years to this one—one more guy even more volatile and moody than the last. At least the last boyfriend didn't do the silent treatment—he was too busy yelling.

I think about that relationship, two years back. I wonder if he's found someone willing to yell in return.

"Do people get married so they've got someone locked in to fight with?" I ask the Spanish moss draped overhead.

Maybe I'm the one who doesn't get it. *Arguments as a form of sharing, at least in their view.*

Maybe they're actually surprised when I walk away, stunned that I don't know how to play, don't act interested at all in the game.

It's always seemed like a waste of time and effort to me.

Of course, the silent treatment is even worse.

Miles assured me that it wasn't me. At least he did that much.

But I had given him plenty of time to process whatever the problem was. Or tell me what was bothering him. Instead he closed me out and walked away.

My work shifts are spent hearing people who are afraid, in pain and suffering. People who are terrified of their own mortality, shocking or screaming, dealing with a level of agony they didn't know was possible.

So I find myself without the capacity to listen to suffering in my free time, especially from people who are healthy and successful and just want someone to listen to them wallow in it.

Maybe I've reached a level of callousness that is sucking the empathy from me. But I know that's not true.

"Make me laugh," I order the breeze as if it's my next lover.

"Make me laugh because that's all I have left to give."

Chapter 16

I sit in the balcony of the First Union African Baptist Church, established in 1881.

The door was open, the lights off.

The ceiling fans are still. It is very, very quiet.

I haven't encountered anyone else from the golf cart group. But then again, I haven't been trying.

The truth is, I like being alone. Chatty small talk hurts my head. I like to be alone with my thoughts, or my non-thoughts, when I release my brain from the structure of words and language.

And that's where I find myself now—unplugged. I don't have words forming in my head. There's no running dialogue of what's happening. No voice-over commentator making observations about my life.

I sit and look around the church.

The beadboard paneling and the clean white banisters at the pulpit refresh me. I am content to be here for as long as I feel like it.

When I arrived, I read the plaque that said it was the site of the Praise House for Mary Field's plantation. The chandeliers of the church were imported from England, the floors are heart pine and the pews are hand carved. The church had been restored in 1998.

I had tried out the hand-carved pews downstairs and admired the lights when I first entered.

But when I saw the rickety staircase to the choir loft, I answered the call, climbing up past wavy panes of old windows.

The loft has not been used except for storage for a decade at least. The whole thing leans down into the church. I hope my weight won't cause its collapse but I don't really care. My fatigue has returned, settling around me like a heavy fog.

I rest my palms on the railing and breathe in the cool, dark air of the building.

Chapter 17

Mesmerized, I don't hear the door open.

"Elizabeth?"

I jump at the sound of my name.

It's Miles.

I can't decide whether to answer or duck and hide. My knees tremble at my indecision.

I set my jaw stubbornly and choose to respond. "Miles."

My knees should not be trembling. I'm not the one who stopped talking. I'm not the one who turned into a different person and became petulant or angry or sad without explanation.

I'm the one who gave him a chance to recover. And when that failed, I went in search of my own happiness. Because he wasn't my problem then and he isn't my problem now.

"Where are you?" he asks.

"In the choir loft."

He moves out from under the balcony and turns to

look up at me.

I know he's going to say something and I'm pretty sure I don't want to hear it.

"What happened?" He says it half as a question and half as a statement.

I look at him for a moment, assessing what is the truth. "We stopped having fun."

He measures his words. "Life isn't always fun."

"No. But I work all day long with shattered bodies and dead babies and long howls of pain. I want the other piece of my life to be different from that."

He tilts his head and watches me. "What do you do?"

"I'm an ambulance paramedic."

"Oh," he says.

And then he sits down.

He looks around the church but doesn't say anything more.

I watch him from my chair in the choir loft. I watch him turn his head. I watch him sag wearily into the hand-carved wooden pew.

I can tell he wants me to come down.

And I'm in no hurry. I've never liked these kinds of conversations, the one that's about to take place.

A minute ticks by. Then two and then five.

I don't come down and he waits patiently.

I'm gauging him, assessing what kind of person he is and what he might mean to me.

I could tell him to go. Or I could remain in the choir loft until he leaves on his own. I could go down and out the door and never look back. I could listen to what he has to say and wish him good luck with his life. Or I could hear what he has to say and spend the rest of my life with him.

Who knows what life brings in each moment?

Being human is so simple and so complicated. Everything can stay the same or change forever in the blink of an eye.

Chapter 18

And because I know just how short and fleeting life can be, I walk down the stairs and stand in front of him.

"I lost my daughter," he says.

I don't know what this means and I don't even know if it's true but I touch him anyway. I put my hand on his arm resting on the back of the pew.

His skin, overlaying his strong forearm muscles, sends a shockwave into my fingers.

He doesn't move or look at me.

"Her mother took her. To Mexico."

He shivers and I wrap my fingers around his forearm and squeeze.

"I was officially notified of her death six weeks ago."

Now he is my problem because I believe him and because his skin is electric.

I move into the pew and sit beside him, taking his hand and interlacing my fingers in his. I follow his gaze to the shafts of sunlight drifting through the window and across the pulpit. I don't look at him as he speaks. I watch the dust motes in the sunbeams as he tells me.

"Her mother, April, ran off with a man. She took Kerri with her. Kerri was two."

I picture the child standing in a sundress, looking for all the world like Miles.

"We were separated. She was living in Savannah. I didn't even know she was gone until a mutual friend called me. Told me she'd packed up and left. Didn't tell anyone where she was going."

The building is deeply silent, as if listening to his words also.

"I did everything I could to find to find her, to find them. It was a nightmare. She had no family. Her friends didn't even know the last name of the guy. Just his first name—Roy. She dropped off the face of the earth."

Time stands still, without even the ticking of a clock.

"I got the call. The local police were notified through channels. International channels somehow. They had driven into Mexico, down to the Yucatan Peninsula. Rented a hut on the beach. And then money got tight and the drinking escalated. Roy started with the abuse. The Mexican police had a couple of reports."

My stomach tightens. *Here it comes*, I think.

"And one night, late, there was a lot of drinking. And Kerri wandered away from the hut. No one noticed her. She washed up the next morning."

Miles stares at the ray of sunlight slanting across the sanctuary. He doesn't blink.

I have seen dead babies. But they weren't mine.

"Why didn't April call me, just call me?" he says in anguish.

I have no answers and there is nothing to say. We both know that. This is a path only he can walk.

Chapter 19

"I can't save you," I finally say. "I can barely save myself."

"I know that," he says.

We sit silently until the sound of gasoline-powered gulf carts announces the disruption of our privacy.

We look at each other, knowing we can't bear the impending chatter.

Without letting go of our handhold, we slip out the side door and hide in the shade of the trees. When the boisterous couples disappear into the church, we sneak toward our carts.

When grief becomes too heavy, the body looks for balance, demands it. The body compensates by finding lightness, an opposing force to the weight.

It's why visitations and wakes often end up in laughter as funny stories, inappropriate as they might seem. It accounts for the dark humor of death-workers—funeral directors, hospice nurses, paramedics.

Something lifts inside of us as we skulk like secret agents toward our getaway vehicles.

We're snorting with laughter, muffling chokes of hilarity one step removed from the ghastly.

Miles makes it worse by singing the James Bond

theme song. We slide into our carts, turn the keys, and roar away haplessly at underpowered speed.

Because the human body can only stand so much grief.

Life is horrible. And life is beautiful beyond belief.

I savor the island wind in my hair.

Miles admires the Spanish moss draping our passage as if he's never really seen it before. His eyes shine as shadows lengthen in the day.

I whoop and he joins me, howling like a wolf. I respond by yipping like a coyote.

It is silly and unsuitable but it's a switch our bodies have thrown when they couldn't handle any more.

We are drunk on the elixir of being alive and all that it means—the deepest of sorrow and the peaks of joy.

Leaving a cloud of dust behind us, we race down the road at fifteen miles an hour.

Chapter 20

The movement of a bird catches my eye.

He's doing something unusual—holding his wings out without flapping.

I slow down to get a better look.

He stretches his neck to one side and then all the way to the other. And then he does it again, without folding his wings or flying away.

I slow to a complete stop. I've never seen anything like this.

Miles circles back, an expression of concern on his face that I might have broken down.

I signal with my head toward the bird.

Miles' glance follows and he breaks into a grin. He pulls his cart next to mine, driver's side to driver's side.

I don't want to say anything. Asking what the bird is doing seems as ridiculous as what the bird is doing.

I can tell Miles has shifted his gaze from the bird to me. My cheeks start turning red from his attention. I loosen my grip on the steering wheel because my palms begin to sweat.

I watch the antics of the bird and smile, partly because of the silliness of the bird and partly because of the silliness of my body's response to

Miles' gaze.

We've been through more in three hours than most people in three weeks of dating. I wonder if it's the effect of the island--the condensing of time and space.

Miles makes a noise with his lips and tongue that causes the bird to look sharply in our direction and jump on a log.

"Do you speak bird?" I whisper to him.

"One of my many talents."

He makes the birdcall again. I watch his mouth this time and feel a tugging sensation inside my chest cavity.

Oh boy, I think, *I've felt this before and I know what it means.*

Chapter 21

"We're here," he says.

"Here where?"

"Where I live. Want to see it?"

I look with awe at the mansion on Daufuskie Island.

Here? Yes."

"The caretaker unit's in the back." He pulls into the circular driveway of a three-story pillared beach house.

Following him, I park my cart beside his. "Is anyone home?"

"I think the gardener is." He winks at me. "I don't have to do the gardening."

He leads me around the side of the big house to a cozy studio nestled under loblolly pines.

He slides open the glass door and ushers me into his abode. It's messy and charming and everything a beach cottage should be. I love it.

The table and shelves are piled deep with research books and stray papers. I assume it's for the book he's working on, the one he mentioned on the ferry.

The small bed is unmade, tucked into a corner, its pillows and blankets tossed carelessly. For a brief moment I find myself imagining all kind of things in the bed before I realize it's much too narrow for two.

The photographs catch my attention--one in particular of a darling little girl in a sundress. She looks like Miles with dark curls and blue eyes.

He sees me looking at the picture and nods.

This is Kerri.

"Let me show you the big house," he says quietly, taking my hand and leading me outside.

The main house is airy and spacious, with big windows and flowing draperies, high ceilings and marble countertops. It's sumptuous and expensive and altogether too big. I enjoy looking but I prefer the studio.

It's obvious Miles takes pride in maintaining the property.

"Nice, huh?" he asks.

"Absolutely gorgeous.

"I knew you'd like it."

"But I like your house better," I quickly add. And I mean it, genuinely.

He gives me a look that I could interpret at least a dozen ways. I let it pass.

Chapter 22

"The beach is walking distance. Want to see it?"

"Of course!"

We set off toward the grass-covered dunes.

He takes my hand. "Are you okay—with what I told you?"

"Yes. And what I said to you—I didn't mean to sound callous. I'm just so tired. So worn out by the suffering. It's every day. I don't think I can do it anymore."

"There are times when I grieve so hard, I think I'm going to die. But there are longer and longer stretches of peace. Or maybe it's numbness."

"We're such a mess."

"We are, aren't we?"

I squeeze his hand. "Let's run away to the beach."

I pull him up and over the dunes. This is the view I've been waiting for.

The Atlantic Ocean stretches into infinity, the crisp white clouds buffeting an azure sky.

"Oh, Miles."

The sea air fills my lungs and soothes the jagged pieces left unhealed in my heart. The sound of the waves swells me with a hope I can only remember as a child.

I realize I've been lost for years.

A pelican slams clumsily into the water in search of dinner. The gulls soar overhead.

I exhale and it comes out as a moan and then Miles is kissing me. His lips find mine and the intensity sends a blinding flash of white light through my brain.

I know him from somewhere, a thousand years ago or just this morning. It doesn't matter.

He takes my face in his hands and kisses me, long and unrushed.

I begin to find myself in finding him.

He pulls me into him and wraps his arms around me.

I raise my arms to his shoulders, my fingers finding the skin of his neck and the soft curls of his hair.

I feel his heart pounding in his chest and his pulse at my fingertips.

The waves break in the distance. I can hear the gulls crying over the tides.

His breath is hot on my skin and I feel him start to tremble.

I feel the sand under my feet. It vibrates with the motion of the sea.

I am lost in the kiss.

Chapter 23

Daufuskie Island breathes for me because I am breathless. My head spins and my lungs have stopped working of their own accord.

Miles kissing me is all I know—his closeness and the taste of his lips.

He takes me in his arms and holds me with savage tenderness.

"Elizabeth," he says simply.

I pull him to me even tighter. I feel his soft breath in my hair and his words come out in a lilting torrent.

"Elizabeth, stay with me."

The ocean waves fold onto themselves ceaselessly. The sound intermingles with what Miles says.

"We'll take it as slowly as we need to. You can sleep in the main house. We'll just see how it goes."

Somehow I know the big house is his and that he's chosen the cottage for now—for the grieving, for reconstructing his life, for his hour of ruination.

"Give us some time. Time—whether it's a day or a year or forever."

The sound of our hearts is louder than the waves.

"Maybe we can heal what's broken. Or maybe not."

I realize I've been so thirsty for so long. I don't say anything. I close my eyes. I soak in his words, asking myself, asking my body for an answer.

"Just one day," he says. "And then maybe another one. We'll stay by the sea. On Daufuskie. And we won't ask each other questions. And we'll talk when we want to. Quietly. Without judgment. One day. And then maybe another. And we'll see."

I look out across the ocean and I hear it whisper my name.

About the Author —

Described as "half Mary Poppins and half Tasmanian Devil," Carol is an attorney and writer hailing from Leadville. Her life has never been boring. She's the author of 18 books and 23 scripts for stage and screen.

Born in Canada, she hasn't died yet, narrowly dancing past the inevitable on hundreds of occasions. Her last words will be, "Watch this." She's usually on a dirt bike, raft or pair of skis, and if she can't be found outdoors, she's probably baking.

Carol gave birth to two Zen masters, daughter Whitney and son Mike, and was "como la mama" to forty others. She believes that raising good children is the most important thing one can do in life.

Carol attended Wellesley College, Wesleyan University and received her law degree from Washington University in St. Louis.

Her bags are always packed and sightings of her have been reported in New Zealand, Hawaii and the catacombs under Paris. She loves languages and makes passable attempts at French, Spanish, Greek and Navajo—not bad for the daughter of a hard-rock miner with a ninth-grade education.

"Being friends with Carol is like getting a new little red wagon every day."—David Long.

Books:

Nine poetry books--*Loving the Cowboy; Never More Beautiful; Between the Tracks; Poems for New Mexico; Cloud Shadow; Ransoming Summer; Lavish Kisses at Midnight; Ontario;* and *Spring Wheat;*

A biography--*Vegas Dynasty: The Story of Darwin Lamb;*

Three books of free plays for adults, teens and kids titled *Theater Shorts 1, 2 and 3;*

And five novels—*Driving North, Estate and Legacy* and the first three novels in a series--*Fire Drifter 1: Meteor Shower; Fire Drifter 2: Trails;* and *Fire Drifter 3: The Vessel.*

Current projects include a thriller titled *Places to Hide*, a young adult science fiction piece called *Storm Tunnel,* a tribute to the beloved Gwynne Cosgriff (poetry and photography) and Madelyn Tremaine's continuing adventures in *Fire Drifter.*

Scripts:

Meteor Shower

Edge

Guido, My Guardian Angel

Cross Roads

Crystal Carnival

Kill for You

Anorexic Psycho Killers of Leadville

Ice

Dancing in the Sand

Stacy

Missing Pieces

Strawberries, Brooms and Pelicans

Marilyn

Vegas Knights

Snow Scent

Note

Leaving

Vestiges

Dragons in Denver

Ghosts in the Graveyard

Cross Roads

Flamboyant

Driving North

Acknowledgements:

Many thanks to:

My daughter Whitney and son Mike for soldiering on as the Zen Masters in my life;

Dawn Beck for holding up my weight through the process and divining everything techie;

Laurel McHargue and the Cloud City Writers Group for enduring support;

Lem Chesher for the adventure and photographs;

And Tina Erickson Westphal for typing, typing, typing and reading my mind about what goes where.

Photo Credits to Lem Chesher: Pages 30, 47, 48, 67, 85, 101 and 104; other photos to Carol Bellhouse.

CPSIA information can be obtained
at www.ICGtesting.com
Printed in the USA
LVHW081257240120
644710LV00015B/431